BRIGHT
IDEA
BOOKS

THE
Truth ABOUT
LIFE AS A
Princess

by Martha London

CAPSTONE PRESS
a capstone imprint

Bright Ideas is published by Capstone Press, an imprint of Capstone.
1710 Roe Crest Drive
North Mankato, Minnesota 56003
www.capstonepub.com

**Library of Congress Cataloging-in-Publication Data is available on the Library of Congress
website.**
ISBN: 978-1-5435-9065-4 (library hardcover)
ISBN: 978-1-5435-9066-1 (eBook PDF)

Summary: Describes the real lives of princesses, including how they become princesses, work for
their countries, give back to charity, and more.

Image Credits
iStockphoto: asiseeit, 31, XiXinXing, cover; Newscom: Jorge Silva/Reuters, 5; Shutterstock Images:
Chaiwat Subprasom, 6, Deborah Kolb, 25, Featureflash Photo Agency, 10–11, Featureflash Photo
Agency/23, Jade ThaiCatwalk, 26–27, Michael715, 18–19, Rob Marmion, 17, 28, Sergio Monti
Photography, 20, Shaun Jeffers, 14, Twocoms, 12–13, Zixia, 9
Design Elements: Shutterstock Images

Editorial Credits
Editor: Charly Haley; Designer: Laura Graphenteen; Production Specialist: Melissa Martin

All internet sites appearing in back matter were available and accurate when this book was sent
to press.

Printed in the United States of America.
PA99

TABLE OF CONTENTS

CHAPTER 1

THE THAI
Princess

Princess Sirivannavari is the daughter of the King of Thailand. She travels all over the world. She trains horses six days a week. She plays badminton.

She started a fashion line when she was 20 years old. All of these things are part of her life as a princess.

Princess Sirivannavari waved to a crowd during a ceremony at the Grand Palace in Thailand.

Princess Sirivannavari (left) used her cell phone to photograph other Thai royals.

The princess works hard. She often trains her horses in the morning. She works on fashion designs in the afternoon. She also meets with leaders of Thailand.

The princess travels a lot. She connects with designers and athletes. She meets other **royals**. The princess cares about Thailand. She wants people to know more about her country.

CHAPTER 2

BECOMING A
Princess

Princess is a title given to a person. Many princesses are born into their titles. Their families are royal. A princess may become queen someday.

Princess Leonor of Spain was born into her title.

Other princesses marry into royal families. They marry princes.

BECOMING QUEEN

Kate Middleton is married to Prince William of the United Kingdom. William will be king someday. Then Kate will be queen.

Kate Middleton and Prince William got married in 2011.

PRINCESS LESSONS

All princesses have responsibilities. A woman might take lessons before marrying a prince. These lessons teach her how to be a princess.

Princesses have to follow rules. Lessons may teach a princess how to walk, sit, and wave. They may teach her how to dress. Royals in the United Kingdom have rules for everything. There is a royal way to hold a cup of tea.

Princesses Beatrice (left) and Eugenie of the United Kingdom rode in a royal carriage.

Princess Meghan Markle of the United Kingdom greeted people during a visit to New Zealand.

STUDYING AND WORKING

Princesses study different languages. They travel around the world. They meet many different people. Studying languages helps princesses speak to everyone they meet.

Princesses work on things they care about. Being a princess is different for everyone.

FASHION WORK

Several princesses have their own fashion lines. Princess Marie-Chantal of Greece has a line of clothes for children.

CHAPTER 3

THE LIFE OF A
Princess

Sometimes people think life is perfect for a princess. Princesses have a lot of money. They meet famous people. They live in big houses and castles. Princesses can help a lot of people.

But being a princess is a busy job. Princesses have many responsibilities. They are often expected to act certain ways.

Every princess has good days and bad days.

17

Princesses can travel all over the world. They go to many different events. They meet many people. This can be fun and exciting.

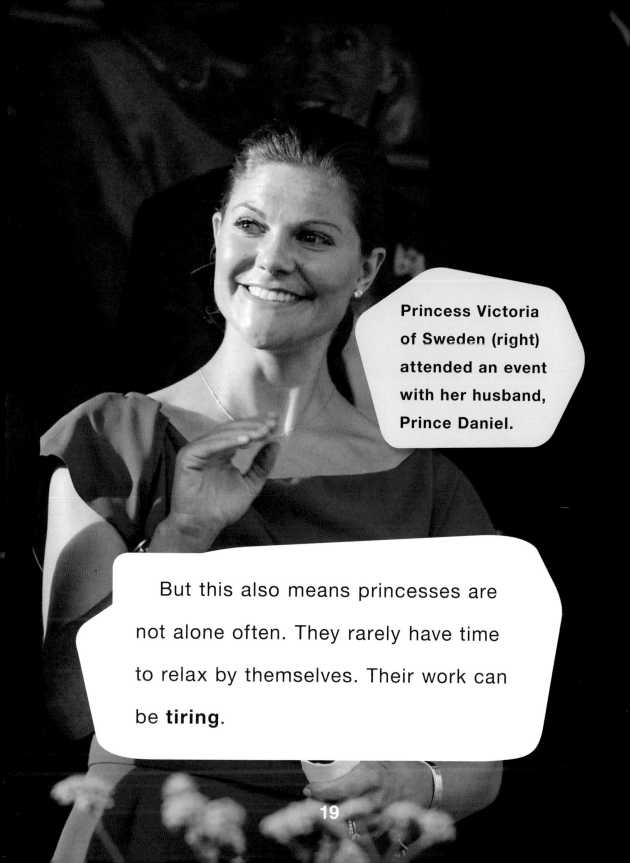

Princess Victoria of Sweden (right) attended an event with her husband, Prince Daniel.

But this also means princesses are not alone often. They rarely have time to relax by themselves. Their work can be **tiring**.

People photographed Princess Charlene Wittstock of Monaco as she attended a fashion show in Italy.

Princesses are always in the **public** eye. Photographers take pictures. Reporters want interviews. Princesses must always be ready to pose and speak.

Being in the public eye is not always easy. Sometimes people say mean things to princesses. But princesses cannot show they are angry or upset.

HELPING OTHERS

Princesses help others. They give time and money to **charities**. Charities work to create a better world. Some charities help people. Others help animals or the **environment**. Charities can raise money to help fight illnesses. Princesses want to help.

Princess Beatrice of the United Kingdom helped answer phone calls at a charity event.

CHAPTER 4

LIKE EVERYONE
Else

In some ways princesses are just like everyone else. They have bad days. They like to see their family and friends. Sometimes they just want to be alone.

Princesses like to have fun like everyone else.

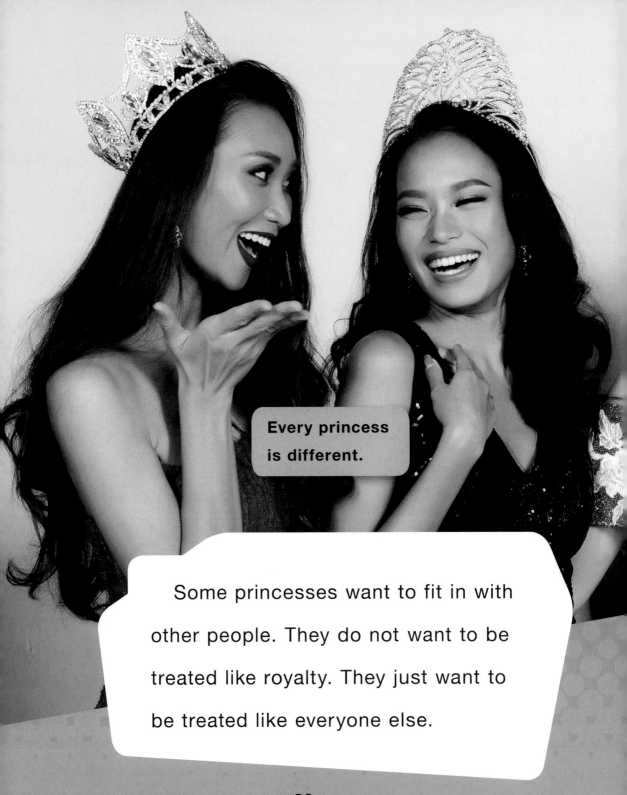

Every princess is different.

Some princesses want to fit in with other people. They do not want to be treated like royalty. They just want to be treated like everyone else.

A RUNNING PRINCESS

Some princesses enjoy sports. Princess Beatrice became the first royal to finish running the London Marathon.

GLOSSARY

charity
a group that works to help a good cause

environment
nature and animals

public
in front of other people

royal
a person in the family that rules a country, such as a king, queen, or princess

tiring
making someone feel tired

TRIVIA

1. **Princess Ameerah Al-Taweel** is a princess of Saudi Arabia. She fights for women's rights in her country.

2. **Rania al-Abdullah** was crowned queen of Jordan in 1999. But before she was queen, she was a princess. She writes books and supports better education for children. She visits the sites of projects that help people to show public support.

3. **Princess Diana of Wales** was called "the people's princess." She was known for being kind.

4. **Meghan Markle** married Prince Harry of the United Kingdom. As a princess, she works toward making sure women are treated equal to men. She also works to make sure people all over the world have clean water.

ACTIVITY

HELP A CHARITY

One of the biggest things princesses do is help charities. These charities are about many different things. Every princess has something she cares about. Princesses give time and raise money to help charities. What is something you care about? Think about how you could help that cause.

There are a lot of groups working to make a difference. Research a charity in your hometown. How can you help? Can you spend time volunteering? Can you help raise money? If there is not a group in your hometown, you can research national charities online. Ask an adult to help you. There are many different ways to give to charity.

FURTHER RESOURCES

Want to learn more about how people become princesses? Check out these websites:

DKFindOut! How Is the British Crown Inherited?

https://www.dkfindout.com/us/more-find-out/special-events/how-is-british-crown-inherited

Wonderopolis: Could You Be Royalty?

https://wonderopolis.org/wonder/could-you-be-royalty

Interested in learning about real-life princesses and queens? Read these books:

Golkar, Golriz. *Meghan Markle*. North Mankato, Minn.: Capstone, 2019.

Heos, Bridget. *Who Wants to Be a Princess: What It Was Really Like to Be a Medieval Princess*. New York: Henry Holt and Company, 2017.

Summers, Portia. *Kate Middleton: Duchess of Cambridge*. New York: Enslow Publishing, 2018.

INDEX